THE POTATO HORSE WHO BECAME A STAR

BASED ON A TRUE STORY!

WRITTEN BY
Samuel Yoder

ILLUSTRATED BY
Brian McCrae

Printed in the United States of America
Published in Hellertown, PA
Cover design, illustrations, and interior design by Brian McCrae
Library of Congress Control Number 2022916533
ISBN 978-1-958711-16-3
2 4 6 8 10 9 7 5 3 1

For more information or to place bulk orders, contact the author or the publisher at Jennifer@BrightCommunications.net.

BrightCommunications.net

To the afflicted,
the marginalized,
who when in power
can change the world

Thank you to my wife, Annemarie,
Catherine, and the true Laura.

CONTENTS

CHAPTER ONE

The Beginning

Fate is a very tricky thing. It can alter one's life in both negative and positive ways. This story begins with two special spirits: one a little Czech girl named Laura, and the other a Haflinger horse named Hany. Little did these two know that they were bound to be united in a powerful relationship that would impact both of their lives.

L aura was born in a very small town named Masecin just outside of the ancient city of Prague in the Czech Republic. She was like any little girl with a joy for life and in awe of the world around her. She grew rapidly, thrived on her parents' love, and began to explore the little farm where she lived.

However, Laura's parents noticed that something was wrong. Laura was falling behind in her ability to speak and learn new words. She was not socializing normally with other little children in the town. Laura's parents took her to the local doctor, and he told them that he believed that Laura was deaf.

Devastated, Laura's parents took her to several hearing specialists at numerous hospitals in the Czech Republic, none providing much hope for a cure. Laura was discouraged and became weary of being shuffled from doctor to doctor. As a last ditch effort to help Laura, she was taken to the best hearing doctor in Europe, near relatives in Flanders, a region in the country of Belgium.

The hearing doctor in Flanders determined that Laura was not totally deaf, but she required a specialized surgery to correct her congenital defect. After the long surgery, Laura COULD HEAR! Sounds she never before perceived flooded into her brain, and she experienced the wonder of this resonating magic.

Hany was a Haflinger horse, a breed of horse developed in the Southern Tyrolean Alps to navigate the rugged terrain of the mountains. Like Laura, he also was born in the Czech Republic on a farm near Prague. The farmer welcomed his birth and was overjoyed to have the addition of a young, spirited colt because he always needed many replacement workhorses for all the fieldwork on the farm.

The farmer specialized in producing delectable potatoes, which needed to be planted, cultivated, and harvested. He used his horses for all these labors, and he loved the nimbleness and level-headed personality of the Haflinger horse. The horses were essential to the operation of the farm because the farmer could not afford to buy a tractor. Hany was destined for a hard life toiling in the fields and probably a shortened life, curtailed because of the wear and tear of everyday work.

From the start, Hany was tethered to his mother
as she worked in the fields. This was Hany's
school. He had to learn how to be a workhorse.
Hany quickly became familiar with the necessary skills
required by a draft horse: pulling alone or in unison
with other horses, backing, going "Gee" or right, going
"Haw" or left, and "Ho" for stopping and standing
without moving around—even if a horsefly bit him
on his leg or back. Hany learned fast, and he was very
talented.

After a couple of years, Hany was ready to join the other horses with their labors under harness. He was excited because this was his destiny, to rotate through generations of horses who grew up to learn, work, and provide the farm with the resources to survive—and eventually to die, physically broken. This was a noble and ancient profession for a horse, and Hany was resigned to enter his predestined role in life.

After several years, Laura finally moved back to her home in the Czech Republic. She had attended special schools in Belgium to catch her up on her speech. Amazingly, she could now speak Flemish, plus also Czech and a little English. She had grown into a young woman of the age of 12 years. She was overjoyed to finally live at the farm she was born at and no longer have to travel back and forth to Belgium for school. It was at this time that she developed an enthusiasm for horsemanship. Her father was a horse trainer, and he was determined to teach Laura how to be a disciplined equestrian.

CHAPTER TWO

The Meeting

One beautiful spring day, Laura and her family were driving in their car to visit a relative in Prague. Laura had just been studying the Greek myths in school and was musing about Mount Olympus, Zeus, Athena, Heracles, and all the mythical characters embodied in those stories. Going down a long country lane that meandered through an emerald valley, Laura was blinded by a golden brilliance created by the sun reflecting off something in the fleeting pasture. *What was it?* Then she saw. It was a beautiful, sorrel chestnut horse with a golden mane and tail. *The mane glowed,* Laura thought, *like the golden fleece in the Greek myth.* "Daddy, look at that horse!!" shouted Laura. "He is magnificent! Who owns him?"

any had also been startled by the amazing feeling he felt when he had locked eyes with the young girl driving past his farm. *She is beautiful! She is magnificent! Who does she belong to?* pondered Hany. But the car raced away before any closure to Hany's thoughts could occur.

L aura's dad had taken notice, and he saw the spark in Laura's eyes as they passed Hany. He had been looking for the right horse for Laura to take lessons on, but his search had ended to no avail.

The next day, Laura's dad drove to the farm where they had seen the horse. He drove down a rugged dirt lane and parked in front of a weather-worn farmhouse. The farmer sidled out to say hello.

"Where is that nice young colt I saw in your pasture?" inquired Laura's dad.

"Which colt?" queried the farmer.

"The one with the glowing mane and tail," exclaimed Laura's dad.

"Oh! You mean my young colt named 'Hany'," exclaimed the farmer.

"Can I see him?" asked Laura's dad.

"Sure," murmured the farmer hesitantly, because he had lots of chores to complete before lunch. "But he's NOT for sale."

Laura's dad followed the farmer into the ancient, medieval barn, down the dusty aisleway, past the sweet smelling hay to a single tie-stall at the end of the barn, and there HE was! Hany was contentedly chewing on his lunch, tied in a stall far away from the other horses.

"Why is he separated?" queried Laura's dad.

"He's my new breeding stallion. Isn't he grand?" proudly chortled the farmer.

Laura's dad introduced himself as the horse trainer who lived down the road, and the farmer was taken aback that this was the famed Czech equestrian he had heard about.

"I need a new horse for the dressage circuit," lamented Laura's dad, whose search had been disappointedly fruitless. Quickly facing the farmer, Laura's dad exhorted him, "Will you not reconsider selling him?"

The farmer was now honored but dumbfounded. He answered, "He is a Haflinger horse, bred for the mountains and the fields…certainly NOT for show."

Laura's dad insisted and inflated the farmer's ego with an overwhelming feeling of pride on how Czechs across the country will know that HE was the farmer who had bred this magnificent colt, especially if he wins his fame. The farmer stepped back. He pondered the offer, drunken with his potential notoriety. "He doesn't come cheap," exclaimed the farmer.

Laura's dad made him an offer he couldn't refuse, and the next day Laura's dad arrived at their farm with the colt safely hidden away in the trailer.

Laura was working in the garden when her father pulled in with the horse trailer at their farm. She was curious why he had the horse trailer hooked up and also why he had left so early that morning.

Laura's mother joined her father at the trailer to inform Laura that they both had a surprise for her. Laura quickly realized that it must be a horse! She ran to the back of the trailer, and her father led the colt with the golden fleece by his halter out for an introduction. Laura and Hany's eyes met, and the magic both had felt that other day in the car was rekindled.

CHAPTER THREE

Kindred Spirits
Become a Team

Hany nuzzled Laura in his new stall. He was entranced with his new young owner. Laura hugged Hany and knew they would be the best of friends. It was late. The stars were shining bright, and the two mused about their dressage future, which surely would be carefree and uncomplicated.

But how wrong they were. Laura's first lessons ended with Laura being bucked off unceremoniously by the exuberant Hany. Hany was like a young, rambunctious teenager, full of fun and play. He thought it was all a game and did not acknowledge that this was school or that he could hurt his new friend Laura. Laura's dad was furious and realized that this potato horse turned dressage horse would require lots of work and a new strategy.

aura's dad decided for Laura to learn the fundamentals of dressage not on Hany, but General: a grey, older horse who had been a seasoned dressage competitor but was retired because of an injury. General was a Kladruber, an ancient Czech breed of horse, who had been trained at the famous Villa Gineta stables for years. He was kind, gentle, and safe and would allow Laura to advance her equestrian skills without worrying about bruising falls.

Meanwhile, Hany was entering a new world of discipline and gymnastics: stretching his neck, stepping backward, crossing his legs, and trying to canter in the shape of a balloon. Hany was initially a rebellious student, resisting his conversion and sometimes even dreaming that the muscle-worn work of a potato horse seemed better. But gradually, Hany began to seriously engage with his new schooling and enjoyed the fleetness and agility that were required for the dancing of a dressage horse.

owever, even with both their advancements in schooling, Hany and Laura had not yet forged that special bond necessary for a dressage team: a bond driven by an imperceivable language to communicate their coordination of command and movement. Horse and rider needed to be one in the ring. Their love for each other was not enough!

 One day, there was a loud thunderclap, an ominous warning of a mid-summer thunderstorm. The blistering heat for days had finally precipitated a massive thunderhead.

Laura was sent to fetch the horses in the pasture before the tempest hit. The winds were building with leaves rustling and tree branches swaying. Laura quickly raced out to the distant field where the horses were stirring and growing restless. She was just about ready to place a bridle on General, when lightning struck and spooked all the horses into a stampede toward the barn.

Unwittingly, because Laura's hearing was not 100 percent, she was caught unaware and was suddenly trapped in a dangerous and torrential storm. Exposed and all alone, Laura called out in fear, "HELP ME!!!"

Close to the barn Hany sensed a danger, not for himself, but for…Laura. Where was Laura? She was still out in the pasture! He wheeled around and raced to rescue his best friend from the dangerous storm. He discovered Laura cowering in the field by a tree, blinded by the blowing rain. He galloped up to her and nudged her, indicating that he was there to help her. Laura blindly reached up, grabbed a handful of Hany's golden mane, and threw herself onto his back. Hany felt her shivering body on his back nestled behind his withers and knew he would always care for and protect this special rider.

Hany turned and galloped back toward the shelter of the barn. He ran swiftly with his precious cargo clinging to his back and turned the corner of the barn, burst through the door, and reached the sanctuary of the medieval barn. He wandered into his stall, bedded thickly with dry straw. They were safe!! Hany, out of breath, was relieved and looked around. All the other horses sheepishly turned their gazes and dropped their heads in shame, even the elder General. However, the storm had initiated a true union. It had galvanized horse and rider, merged the existence of a mere Haflinger potato horse and a young Czech girl. The bond was sealed! They were forever a team.

CHAPTER FOUR

Showtime!

It was a rainy day in October with the show arena immersed in water creating a tenacious mud. Laura's dad had decided that Hany's first competition needed to be deep in the country away from large crowds and the pressure of a large competition. He wanted Hany and Laura to become accustomed to the noises of a show, the dressage ring, and the commotion created by the other competitors and their horses. Many large warmblood horses with experienced older riders mulled around the practice ring rehearsing their tests. Fancy saddles padded with saddle pads adorned with the national flag or embroidered stable name, expensive bridles made of exotic leathers, and dressage outfits of exquisite design adorned Laura's competitors. Laura felt a big knot tightening in her stomach, but she assured Hany not to be intimidated by all this flamboyance.

The weather continued to dole out rain and more rain, creating more and more mud. As each rider and horse took their turn and entered the swampy ring, the big warmblood horses were annoyed and rattled by the mud spilling over their long beautiful legs precipitating mistake after mistake with the ensuing deductions to their scores. Each subsequent contestant faltered in the ring, souring all the disgruntled entries...except one!

When Hany and Laura walked into the show arena, many old farmers and even some of the judges laughed at the young girl with her small, "yellow" horse pretending to be a dressage horse. Whoever could imagine a Haflinger horse being a dressage horse? However, the laughs and more importantly the mud did not faze Hany because he was born to be a potato-digging horse, who thrived in the muddy farmer's fields.

Laura took up the reins and gently nudged Hany into action with her boots. Around the ring they maneuvered, performing their test with precision, perfectly executed and astounding all their now dumbfounded critics. When the results were in, Hany and Laura had taken first place and stunned the crowd. The months of practice and preparation had paid off, and they had proven that they were a winning team! It was a tremendous beginning and an unexpected victory.

But their victory was fleeting. After a winter of rest and a new accelerated training period, Hany and Laura were in top shape for the start of the series of the next year's competitions. They had trained exhaustingly and reached what they thought was their peak performance. During their first competitions, Hany and Laura repeated their success evident in October of the previous year. The winning was sweet. But, little did Laura or her dad know that Hany had other ideas. He had become bored with the repetitive exercises and decided to "spice up" their act. He would show everyone who was the star.

During their next competition, Hany had planned to add some extra moves to "entertain" the crowd. He started bucking playfully during cantering or would come to a sudden halt with Laura being incapable to get him to move again. Other times, he would pirouette during the middle of their performance, arousing the audience to laugh uncontrollably while Laura melted in the saddle with embarrassment.

Hany had forgotten that he was an integral part of a dressage team. Laura was the conductor, and he was the showman—but not a clown. He had reverted to his initial teenage antics.

aura's dad was furious. He had been working with horses since he was a boy of 14 and trained at the renown Kladruber Horse Academy. In the Czech army, he acquired strict discipline, which served him well as the first ever Czech dressage competitor at the European Haflinger Championship in Austria. He decided to outwit Hany and integrate new protocols into their training. He changed part of Hany's feed, no more grain to make him "hot" or bursting with vigor. A new warming-up time was instituted to tire Hany so he no longer had extra energy to entertain the crowd or think of anything beyond his five minutes of competition. Laura's dad used all his expertise to mold Hany into a showman, yes, but a showman who took commands from Laura and not from himself.

After three or four competitions, Hany and
Laura were in the top five competitors again.
They were winning against some of the finest
horses in Europe and advanced to a new level that
caught the attention of the Czech Haflinger Federation.
They asked Laura's dad if Hany and Laura would be
interested in registering for the prestigious European
Haflinger Championship to be held in Italy the following
summer. Everyone was excited and jumped with joy with
this national honor. However, there could be a potential
roadblock: Was Hany a purebred Haflinger?

Hany was a farm potato horse. This characteristic had been an asset in Hany's first competition, but now it was a hindrance to clarifying his true bloodline. The farmer who raised him had died, and there was no resource to answer this all-important question. Without the documentation of ancestry, Hany needed to have a DNA blood test. The farm veterinarian was called, blood was drawn from Hany's neck, and the test was submitted to the lab. Laura and her dad waited nervously for the results. Hany could not understand why everyone seemed so jittery.

Had Hany descended from the long line of agile and sure-footed workhorses from the Southern Tyrolean Mountains in Austria and Italy? The first description of the Haflinger horse as we know it today came from the small Austrian village of Hafling in 1874 when the foundation stallion, 249 Folie, was born of the sire half-Arab stallion, 133 El' Bedavi XXII, who had been crossed with a refined native Tyrolean mare. Folie's father was the great-great grandson of the original imported Arab stallion, El Bedavi. Folie's dam was a chestnut mare, the product of the mating of a Gidran stallion with a local mare. (Gidrans are a heavy Hungarian Arabian half-bred horse.) Was Hany going

to travel back to his forefathers historical lands for the European championship? Only the submitted blood test would give the answer.

Two weeks passed, and finally a letter came in the mail from the Czech Haflinger Federation. Hany could not have more than 1 percent of Arabian genes to be considered a Haflinger for the championship...and he didn't! Hany, the potato horse from the fields of the Czech Republic, WAS a true Haflinger, and he could now enter the show of his life in Italy.

That night, Laura nuzzled Hany, and he knew that she was telling him that something BIG was in their future!

CHAPTER FIVE

The Championship

It was a long, grueling journey. The family and Hany had driven 15 hours from Prague through Germany, past Munich, through Lichtenstein and into Switzerland, over the Alps to Italy where they finally reached the great star-shaped equestrian complex at Vermazzo. Hany was not used to such a long travel-time to a show, and he was not drinking enough water. Laura's dad was getting concerned.

Excitement was at a fever pitch, and the stables were full of commotion and activity. The team from Denmark had a truck with 18 Haflingers, all outfitted with expensive tack and equipment.

The Dutch team had a whole section in the stables decorated with orange and exuded an air of confidence. The team from Germany was ready to highlight their exceptionalism, but it was the Austrian team that everyone was watching.

The Austrians had always claimed the mantle of Haflinger superiority. The Haflinger horse was one of their national horses, shoulder-to-shoulder with the Lipizzaner. The Lipizzaner embodied the noble's horse, descending from the royal Hapsburg Spanish riding school in Vienna. The Haflinger was worshipped by the common man as a sturdy, versatile horse that fulfilled the demands of everyday life. The Austrians could not even imagine that any other country could outdo them in any Haflinger competition.

Hany and Laura were the Czech Republic's only competitor and the only hope for Czech national prestige. This honor was incredible, but it also carried a heavy responsibility, and Laura and Hany felt the pressure. Hany was bedded down for the night in his stall, and they all awaited the next day with full anticipation.

When Laura and her dad arrived at the stable the next morning, Hany was lying down, not hungry and not his usual playful self. Laura's dad immediately called the veterinarian. Hany had a fever and was diagnosed as exhausted and dehydrated from the long trip. Hany's decision not to drink enough water on the trip now had consequences.

The veterinarian gave Hany an infusion of fluids and other medicines. He said only time would tell if Hany would respond. Laura and Hany's competition was in jeopardy and hung in the balance.

Hany rallied after a few hours, and Laura knew he was better after he pulled a handkerchief from her back pocket. The playful, carefree Hany was BACK!!!

Unfortunately, time had been lost, and Hany and Laura had missed their slot to practice in the precompetition training. This was a serious misfortune because they were unable to get a feel for the arena and all the pomp associated with it: flags, colorful billboards, and the resounding echo in a gigantic show arena.

I nstead, Laura and her dad spent this valuable time performing Hany's full preshow preparation. This started with a full body massage, shampooing off the feverish sweat and dirt, and braiding his golden mane into rows of pleated perfection. It was then that Laura pulled out the special saddle pad she had been saving for this competition. The pad was embroidered with the legendary white Czech horse of extraordinary intelligence called Šemík.

Šemík was a horse of Czech legend. His owner was a farmer named Horymír who opposed the greedy prince Křesomysl who was forcing Czech farmers under his rule to abandon their farmlands and dig to mine for gold. Horymír resisted, exhorting his

peers that such a move would lead to famine and subsequently led a valiant farmers' rebellion against the prince's greed.

Unfortunately, Horymír was captured and sentenced to death but given one last wish. He chose to ride his beloved horse, Šemík, one last time. When Horymír mounted Šemík, he whispered in his ear and off raced Šemík, who leaped over the castle's walls and floated down the cliffs and across the Vltava river. Horymír's captors last spied this supernatural pair galloping off triumphantly in the distance toward Prague.

aura believed that the image of Šemík would imbue Hany with the power of that Czech horse. Laura dressed in her competition outfit adorned with the Czech flag and their show number affixed to her back. They were ready, and the pair glowed, shocking the Germans and Austrians who ran to stare at this majestic duo who had just entered the warm-up ring.

It was then that Laura knew that the hardships of their past were now their strongest assets: Hany the potato farm horse and Laura the young Czech girl afflicted with deafness. Laura dismounted Hany and replaced Hany's show bit with the work bit he had used on the potato farm. Hany tasted the earth from his Czech farm as a foal, and the stream of memories created a surge of power to permeate his body.

Laura remounted and removed the battery from the device necessary for her to hear. She was now deaf again, connected to Hany by her barely perceptible signals alone. Hany was again the Czech potato horse from Prague attuned to the subtle movements from the farmer's reins.

Their time to perform was called, and Laura's dad motioned to her to move to the arena, confused why she had not heard the announcement. Laura and Hany entered the gigantic arena, and Laura leaned over Hany's neck and whispered in his ear just like Horymír whispered in Šemík's ear. Hany knew what to do. Laura was not distracted by the eruption of noise in the stadium. She and Hany were one, a team forged from adversity, now ready to begin the competition of their lives.

CHAPTER SIX

A Warm and Pleasant Feeling

Laura walked to the barn and started her daily routine to ride Hany. She fed Hany and the other horses and maneuvered her way to the tack room. She gathered her saddle, saddle pad, and bridle and placed them on the timeworn stand sitting in the aisle near Hany's stall. Today she would give Hany a day off from training and ride him in the freshly cut hay fields and pastures.

In the tack room, Laura noticed the special saddle pad emblazoned with the picture of Šemík, the pad she had used in Vermazzo at the championship. A warm and pleasant feeling permeated her body as she recalled that event. She remembered that day as clearly as yesterday.

She recalled leaning over Hany's neck and whispering in his ear, "We are a winning team, Hany, and you and I can DO IT!" They then entered the arena at a beautiful, relaxed, sitting trot and slowly but elegantly circled the arena till they stopped in the center and bowed in front of the judges who were stationed in a booth. How excited she felt at that moment even though she was extremely nervous.

Laura pulled Hany out of the stall, placed him in the cross-ties, and removed his blanket. She proceeded to pick out his feet and brush out all the dirt and dried sweat from his body, mane, and tail. How handsome he is! Back in Vermazzo, he had shocked the arena with his lithe muscles and perfect Haflinger line.

Laura reminisced how she cued Hany to move-out and start their advanced and difficult test. She had entered the championship at the most difficult dressage level and whispers had permeated the event wondering how such a young Czech girl and her horse could accomplish such difficult maneuvers. The lights, the crowd of spectators, and the smells of that moment rebounded in her head.

Laura remembered how she leaned and Hany turned. She fixed her eyes on a spot, and that's where he went. They performed collected and extended trots and cantors with precision, and their half pass and shoulder-in were exceptional.

She placed the wraps and bell-boots on Hany's legs and braided his beautiful golden mane. She placed the saddle pad and saddle on his back and tightened his girth strap. She grabbed his bridle and recollected how precarious it was to have switched out his broken snaffle bit for his old work bit at the championship, but Hany knew why she did it, and he had felt a resurgence of power when he recalled his humble farm beginnings.

Laura recollected how she had imperceptibly asked him to perform a flying lead change, executed like flying Pegasus, the horse of fame from the Greek myths.

She unsnapped the cross-ties and placed the bit of the bridle in his mouth. She walked outside into the bright, warm sunshine, and they both inhaled the fresh air of the country. She unlatched the gate to the fields and pastures, and they walked to a level spot.

How they had grown to be true kindred spirits! She mounted Hany, and they walked toward the lush, dew-covered fields.

Laura felt like she was at the championship again. She recalled with pride how they perfectly performed their last move, the piaffe, where the horse, in a highly collected fashion, performs a cadenced trot in place. The crowd had been spellbound, and Laura knew at that moment they had astonished the spectators and judges alike. She recalled finishing their program bowing to the

judges and knowing they had been exceptional!

Laura remembered the thrill she felt when they had won the championship when the medal and ribbon were nestled around her neck. Hany also got a ribbon and a medal, and Laura recalled how the arena erupted in applause and acclaim at their victory. Yes, how amazing it was that a deaf girl from Prague had risen to become a champion! But even more miraculous was how a potato horse from humble beginnings had truly BECOME A STAR!

Glossary

Bridle: The headgear used to control a horse by a rider or driver. It consists of buckled straps to which a bit and reins are attached.

Canter: The three-beat gait of a horse. It is smoother and slower than a gallop.

Collected trot: A pace with shorter steps and an uphill balance to the horse's movement

Dressage: The execution by a trained horse of precision movements in response to barely perceptible signals from its rider. The art of riding and training a horse in a manner that develops obedience, flexibility, and balance

Equestrian: noun: A rider or performer on horseback
adjective: relating to horse riding

Extended trot: A pace that shows the maximum length of stride, frame, and phase of suspension in a horse's movement

Flying lead change: The horse changes its lead (or dominant leg) while staying at the canter

Gidran: A Hungarian Anglo-Arab horse breed developed in Hungary from bloodstock that includes the Arabian horse. All members are chestnut in color. It is an endangered breed today with only about 200 horses alive worldwide.

Haflinger horse: A short, compact horse originating from the Tyrolean area of Austria and northern Italy. It is known for its beautiful, golden color and cream or white colored mane and tail. Haflingers are people oriented and have a sweet, laid-back temperament, making them the ideal family horse.

Half pass: A movement in dressage where the horse moves forward and sideways at the same time. The horse should be bent in the direction he is traveling.

Kladruber: The oldest Czech horse breed and one of the world's oldest horse breeds. They are very rare and are bred to be a heavy type of carriage horse.

Piaffe: A dressage movement where the horse is in a highly collected trot standing in one place and not moving forward

Saddle pad: A cushioned pad or blanket laid under the saddle to protect the horse's back

Shoulder-in: A dressage movement where the horse's shoulder is brought to the inside while the hind end stays along the wall

Sorrel: A reddish coat color in a horse lacking any black. Often synonymous with chestnut

Southern Tyrolean Alps: A mountain range in south Central Europe extending over 650 miles from south of France to Slovenia

Tack/tack room: The equipment needed to ride or drive a horse. / The room where the horse's tack is kept to keep it clean and dry

Warmblood horse: An athletic horse that is a cross of a cold, large draft breed with a smaller, quicker hot horse breed. They are typically intelligent with a calm temperament.

Withers: The highest point of a horse's back, lying at the base of the neck above the shoulders. The height of a horse is measuring at the withers.

About the Author

Samuel Yoder, VMD, grew up on a small farm in rural Pennsylvania and became intrigued by the uniqueness and beauty of all animals. He attended high school in Kutztown, Pennsylvania, and earned a bachelor of science in chemistry and biology at Muhlenberg College in Allentown, Pennsylvania. Graduating from veterinary school at the University of Pennsylvania in 1986 set into motion 35 years and counting of the care and treatment of all sorts of animals in private practice with his wife and partner, Annemarie Yoder, DVM. He presently lives and farms on a certified organic farm called Green Alchemy, operated completely sustainably with solar PV, wind, and biofuels. He is currently pursuing a master's degree in anthropology at the University of Pennsylvania and enjoys studying past civilizations.

About the Artist

Brian Keith McCrae, the illustrator, lives in Northern Vermont where he teaches art at his old high school. He has a bachelor's degree in fine art from the University of Vermont and also a degree in digital graphic art. He also studied art history and archaeology at the University of Edinburgh, Scotland. Currently, as a part of his school's Arts and Communications Academy, he works with his students to acquire skills in traditional drawing and painting, ceramics and sculpture, as well as digital photography, graphic design, and video.